Wanda and the alien were best friends.
As a special birthday treat, the alien was taking
Wanda home to his planet for a space party!

While the little rocket whizzed through space, Wanda and the alien didn't get bored.

They painted pictures,

made up funny songs,

practised dancing,

and had lots of tea parties.

The alien even taught Wanda...

...how to speak Space!

But mostly they just gazed out of the window.

Space was **amazing!**

Finally they landed…

...on the alien's planet.

There were so many things that the alien wanted Wanda to see. First he showed her the tallest building.

It was so tall it peeped up above the clouds.

Wanda was too excited to sleep.
She couldn't stop thinking about her party...

the birthday cake,

the party hats,

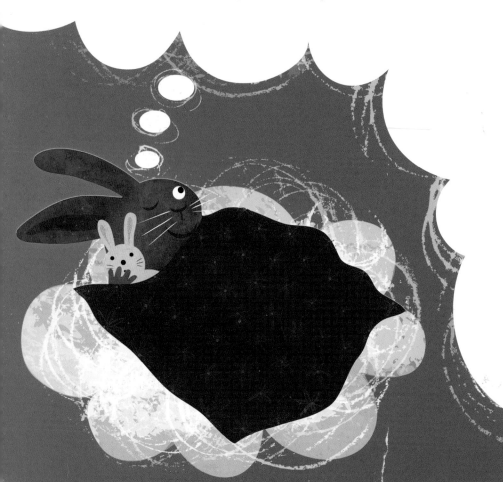

the party food,

the presents,

the cards,

**the party games,
like pass the parcel,**

and the decorations…

The alien couldn't stop thinking about Wanda's party either...

the birthday cake,

the party hats,

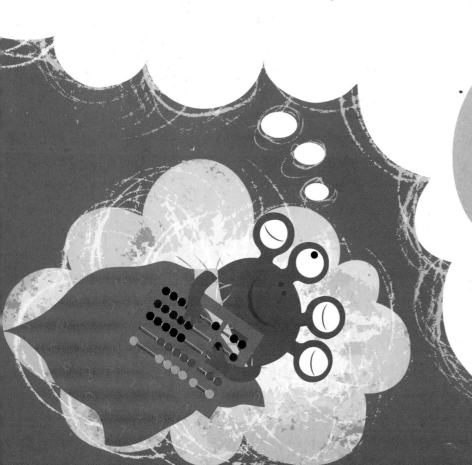

the party food,

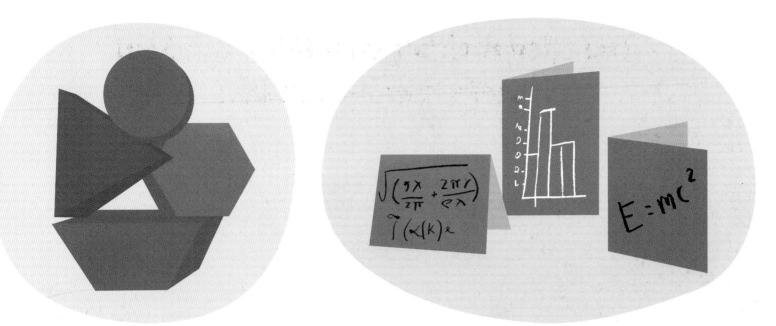

the presents,   **the cards,**

and the party games, like who can be quiet the longest!

He wanted to give Wanda the **best** birthday party she'd ever had.

When Wanda woke up it was her birthday and she was very excited.

The alien was very excited too.
"Come on, Wanda!
It's time for your…"

Without a word,
Wanda turned and left.
Didn't she like her party?

Wanda walked

and walked...

**all the way back
to the rocket.**

**As far as she was concerned there was something
very wrong with this party.**

It needed some music!

As the music played,
Wanda and the alien gazed up
at the stars.

"This is the **best** party I've ever had.
Thank you!" whispered Wanda.
The alien planet was starting
to feel just like home.

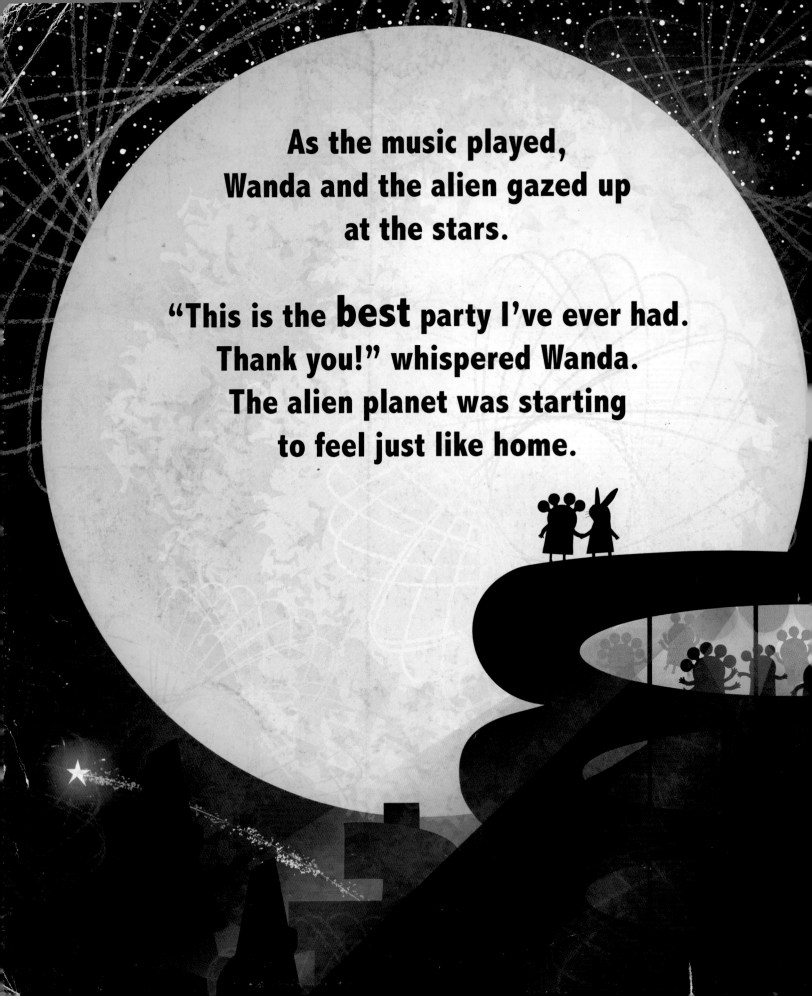

For my son, the Herbie-saurus. G.P.J.

For my son, the Codie-opteryx. G.P.

This paperback edition first published in 2015
by Andersen Press Ltd.
First published in Great Britain in 2014
by Andersen Press Ltd.,
20 Vauxhall Bridge Road, London SW1V 2SA.
Published in Australia by Random House Australia Pty.,
Level 3, 100 Pacific Highway, North Sydney, NSW 2060.
Text copyright © Gareth P. Jones, 2014.
Illustrations copyright © Garry Parsons, 2014.
The rights of Gareth P. Jones and Garry Parsons to be
identified as the author and illustrator of this work have
been asserted by them in accordance with the
Copyright, Designs and Patents Act, 1988.
All rights reserved.

Printed and bound in Malaysia.

1 3 5 7 9 10 8 6 4 2

British Library Cataloguing in Publication Data available.

ISBN 978 1 78344 167 9

The DINOSAURS are HAVING a PARTY!

Gareth P. Jones

Garry Parsons

ANDERSEN PRESS

The dinosaurs are having a party
It starts precisely at three
But I'm a boy not a dinosaur
So I'm pleased they've invited me.

The dinosaurs are having a party

It isn't too far on the bus

The house is vibrating and shaking

But the neighbours aren't making a fuss.

A **big** dinosaur **appears** by the **door**

He **smiles** and says **"Hello.**

There are **plenty** of **meat eaters** in here
Are you **sure** you want to go?"

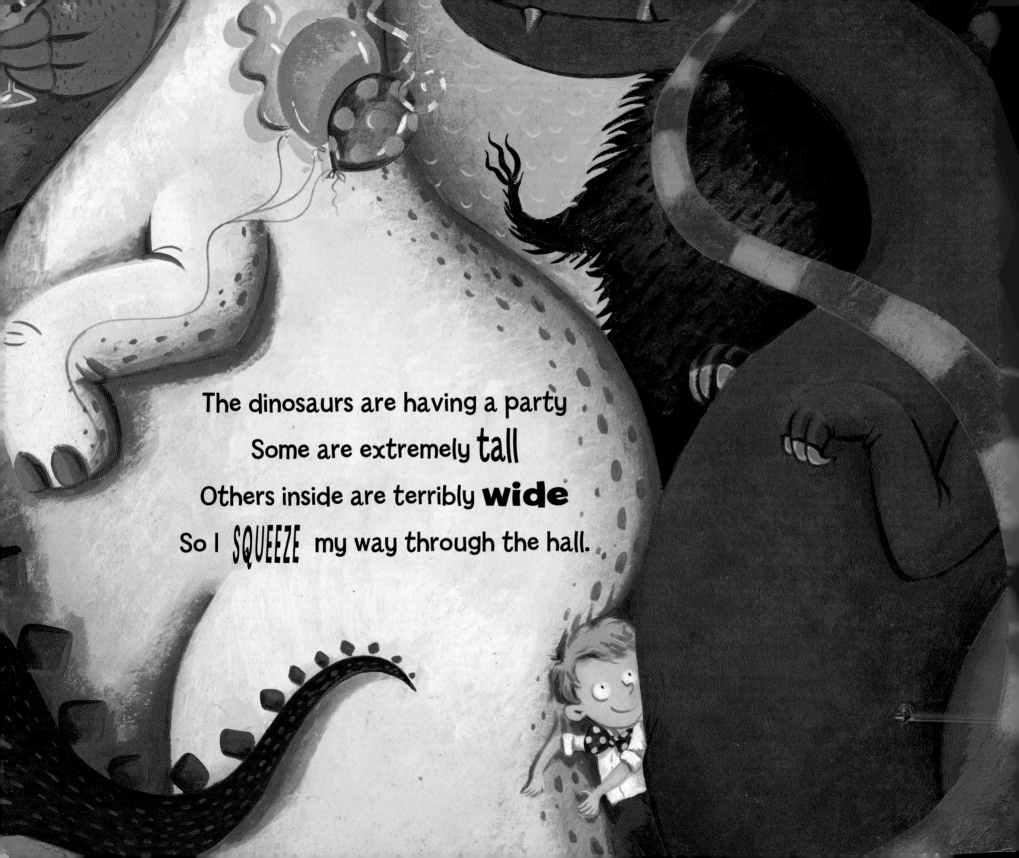

The dinosaurs are having a party
Some are extremely **tall**
Others inside are terribly **wide**
So I SQUEEZE my way through the hall.

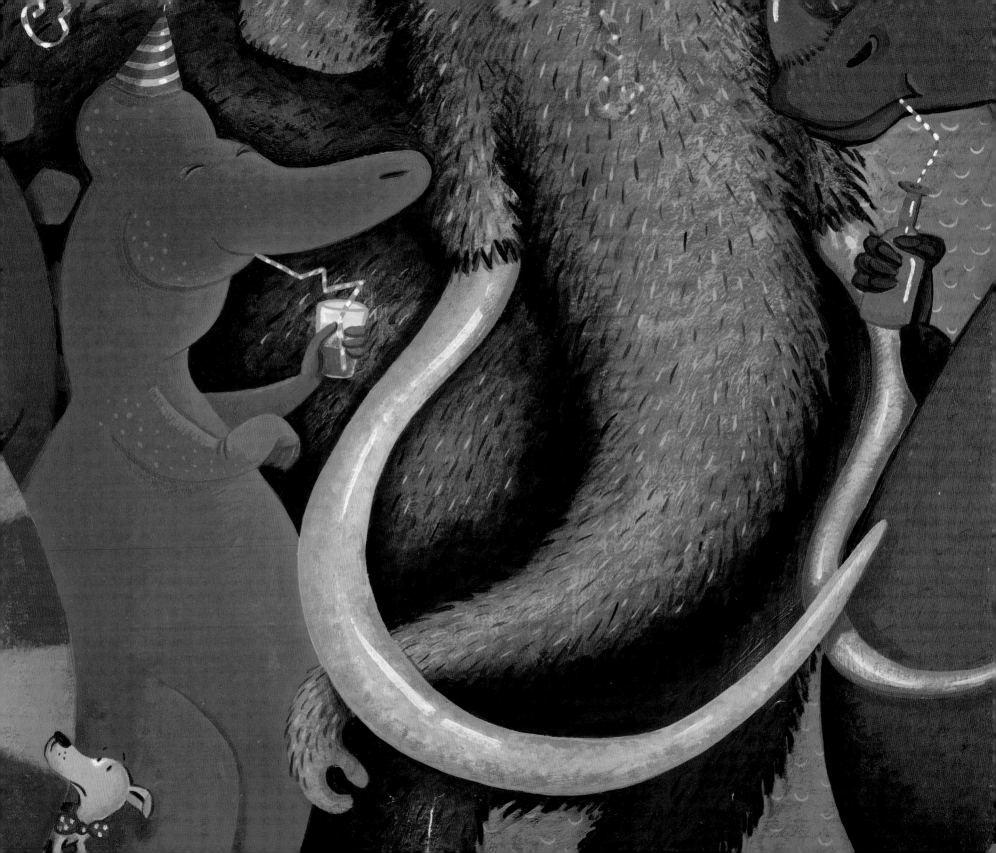

Stepping inside one of the rooms
There's a game of musical chairs
A little one loses and wails,
"Not fair! Nobody cares!"

So they change instead to musical **bumps**

The music suddenly stops

The little one looks like he's winning...

Till he's **squished** by a **triceratops.**

The dinosaurs are having a party

There's plenty of food to gobble

There are jellies of every flavour

Though something is making them wobble.

There's a barbecue in the back garden

Though I can't see a morsel of meat

The cook suggests I sit down

But I don't like the look of the seat.

The bouncy castle is lots of fun
For the whole of the dinosaur gang
Until a **huge** stegosaurus **jumps** on

And **bursts** the **whole thing** with a **BANG!**

There's a really long queue for the toilet

Someone is being too slow

One desperate dinosaur's shouting,

"Hurry up. We all need to go!"

T-Rex steps out with a

Roar!

I go to grab a party bag

I've had such a lot of fun

But T-Rex spots me sneaking out

So I break into a RUN.

The driver turns left,

then right,
then left

Trying his best
to confuse him.

I mostly enjoyed the dinosaurs' party

There is just one little snag.

I don't think the bag I picked up...

Was really a PARTY BAG!

Daddy!